JAXON

ALL THE SINGLE DADS BOOK ONE

SADIE KING

LET'S BE BESTIES!

A few times a month I send out an email with new releases, special deals and sneak peeks of what I'm working on. If you want to get on the list I'd love to meet you!

You'll even get a free short and steamy romance when you join.

Sign up here:
www.authorsadieking.com/free

ALL THE SINGLE DADS

These single dad hotties are fiercely protective and will do anything for the ones they love.

The series features grumpy single dads, secret billionaires, shy neighbors, and men turned obsessive by the curvy heroines who capture their hearts.

Each book in the series is a standalone but best enjoyed together. And look out for your favorite characters from Maple Springs popping in for cameo appearances.

All the Single Dads

Jaxon – Kali & Jaxon

Jake – Fiona & Jake

Levi – Aria & Levi

Brock – Olive & Brock

Anton – Eden & Anton

Xavier – Angela & Xavier

Maple Springs

Small Town Sisters

Candy's Café

All the Single Dads

Men of Maple Mountain

JAXON

ALL THE SINGLE DADS BOOK ONE

She's a hot mess, he's a billionaire in need of a nanny...

Kali

I'm working in yet another dead-end job when Mr. Handsome himself offers me a position as his live-in nanny.

His mansion is luxurious and elegant, and I'm way out of my comfort zone.

He only has one rule: Don't make a sound.

Which is kind of hard for a girl who loves to sing.

And when he takes that rule into the bedroom, it might just be my undoing.

Jaxon

My son is the most important thing in my life, and he needs a nanny.

When I spontaneously employ the deliciously curvy Kali, I don't expect to be as captivated by her as my son is.

She's joyful, authentic, and innocent. She fills the house with song and brings laughter to my heart.

But I swore I'd never let another woman into my

life. I'm damaged goods, and she deserves better than that.

Jaxon is a single-dad age-gap instalove romance featuring an OTT obsessed hero and the young curvy woman he claims as his own.

1

JAXON

I tap my fingers against my beer and resist the urge to check my phone. I don't want to be here listening to men talk about how to deal with toddler tantrums, but my little brother Xavier has set up this single dads support group, so I've come along to support him.

Sure, I'm the single dad of a two-year-old, but there's only one way I deal with tantrums, and I don't think the liberal dads standing around the bar want to hear it.

"You want another beer?" I ask Xavier.

He shakes his head. "Nah man, I'm driving."

It's useless to try to tell him that two beers over the course of the evening won't put him over the limit. My brother errs on the side of caution, always.

I wander over to the bar just as the conversation turns to screen time.

"What can I get you, dude?" the pimply bartender asks.

I wave my bottle in front of him. "Another beer."

While I wait for my drink, I lean on the counter and look around The Blue Boar, Maple Springs's only bar.

It's a Tuesday night, and the place is almost empty aside from the group of tired dads in the corner.

There's movement by the side door, and I watch a woman struggle with an overflowing trash bag. She's dragging it along the floor, and there must be a hole somewhere because she's leaving a trail of dirty liquid behind her.

But that's not what catches my attention. The dim light of the bar shows the contours of her curvy figure. Her black bartender's skirt hugs a generous ass, and as she leans forward to adjust the bag, her blouse falls open. I catch a glimpse of the crevasses of her cleavage thrown into shadow by the low light.

Just then the side door opens, and a short man with a bald head who's wearing a sweat-stained shirt comes through.

He throws his hands in the air and says something in a sharp tone that I don't catch. I'm guessing it's about the liquid spilling onto the floor.

She frowns and checks the floor as he gives her a dressing down. He must be the manager, and it seems to me that he's overreacting. He looks like one of those guys who's perpetually cross.

As he walks away, she gives him the finger behind

his back, which makes me chuckle. Good to see she has some fight in her.

The bartender sets my beer down in front of me, and by the time I finish paying, the woman has gone.

I head back to the dad group where the discussion had turned to schools. I should pay attention; Daniel is my sole responsibility now that his useless mother up and left.

"Where will you send Daniel?" Jake asks.

Jake's the younger brother of a good friend of mine and has been stuck with his little girl to look after permanently. He looks tired and ragged and anxious. And this is why Xavier started the group. Because not everyone is as lucky as I am and able to throw money at the problem.

"I'm sending him to private school."

Jake raises his eyebrows. "Like boarding school? You'd be able to part with him?"

I think about the toddler tantrums, the sleepless nights, and I nod. "Yeah. Better for both of us."

"I couldn't send Riley away, not in a million years."

He rubs a hand through his unkempt hair, and I wonder, not for the first time, if I'm missing something.

I love my son, but I also love my own life and sleep, and if I'm going to prep him to take over my business one day, he needs the best private school education he can get.

A hand claps down on my shoulder, and I turn to see Xavier grinning.

"How's the latest nanny working out?"

My nanny left two days ago for reasons I still can't fathom. I work from home, and all I ask is for complete silence during working hours, from her and my son. I must have told her a hundred times to keep him quiet or take him out. I thought it was a reasonable request, but she didn't like being given the feedback.

"She left."

Xavier clicks his teeth. "Another one down, brother? What are you doing to scare them away?"

"If someone can't take constructive criticism, then they've got no business working for me."

He shakes his head, the good-natured grin never leaving his face. "Can I give you a bit of constructive criticism?"

"No."

"Lighten up."

I give him a scowl that would make my business partners quake, but it doesn't even register with my brother.

"You need help more than they need a job, so go easy on the next one."

"There's not going to be a next one."

He raises his eyebrows at me. "Who's going to look after Daniel?"

"I'm looking after him."

His eyebrows shoot even further up his head. "What do you mean?"

"He sat in his playpen quite happily today while I worked."

"All day? Didn't he cry?"

"I don't know. I had my noise cancelling headphones on."

His face falls. "You can't do that."

"I can and I did. None of the nannies I've had have been up to the task of raising my son. I'll do it myself."

"You can't. You need help. He needs stimulation and feeding and his diaper changed."

He looks panicked, and I almost give up the ruse. I'm not as heartless as I like to make out.

The truth is that since the nanny left, I cancelled all my meetings and have spent the last three days hanging out with my son. My designer sweatpants are covered in baby food, and the house is a mess.

I've taken him to the park, made him bolognaise, read him stories, and built a train set with him. It's been some of the happiest days of my life, but also hard, so hard.

And I can only stay away from my business dealings for so long. My brother's right. I need help.

"I suppose you're right," I say with a sigh.

I look around the bar, and my gaze alights on the waitress I saw earlier. She's leaning against the bar, and her skirt's riding up the back of her thick thighs. As I watch, the manager comes up behind her. He brushes past her a little too close, and his hand shoots out and runs over her ass.

I feel a flash of anger course through me, and my fists clench.

She spins around, her mouth hanging open in indignant surprise.

"Did you just touch my ass?"

The manager puts his hands in the air. "Sorry. It was an accident."

Her eyes narrow, and I'd hate to be on the receiving end of that look.

"It was not, you dirty little man."

He holds his hands up. "Easy girl. You want to keep your job, you'd better watch your mouth."

"And you'd better keep your hands to yourself, asshole."

His face turns so red I think he's going to pop a vein. "That's it. You're fired."

"Fine. I don't want to work here with some creepy old man anyway. Haven't you heard of the MeToo movement? Dickhead."

She unties her apron and throws it on the bar. I like her courage and her ability to stand up for herself. She looks like she could hold her own working in my household.

I set my beer down on the table.

"I've just found my new nanny."

2

KALI

"I must be freakin' crazy," I mutter to myself as I stare up at the three-story mansion before me. I shield my eyes against the sun glancing off the white brickwork.

It's got thick columns like some kind of Ancient Greek palace and a row of carefully sculpted trees line the wide driveway. My beat-up little Nissan hatchback looks out of place against the extreme elegance. I didn't even know places like this existed in Maple Springs. It's right on the edge of town with a good view of the mountains.

As my footsteps echo on the marble stairs, (seriously, who has marble stairs leading up to their front door?) I wonder if I've made a huge mistake.

I think back to the night before when I'd just told Steve, the bar manager, where to go.

Behind my bravado I was silently freaking out,

wondering what the hell I was going to do for work and if I'd ever get enough money together to move out of my parents' place. Then a tall, dark stranger sauntered over and offered me a nanny job.

Like, what? As he was telling me the merits of his son and why I should come and work for him, I was transfixed by his face. Wondering how he got his hair to fall in perfect thick waves and why a man needs such full lips.

I agreed to the job mainly to spite Steve.

But now that I'm here and about to lift the ridiculously heavy brass knocker, I wonder what I was thinking.

I've never nannied before. Sure, I've babysat a few times, but not all day for a two-year-old. I did explain this to Mr. Handsome, but he just stared at me with intense green eyes and told me I'd gotten the job.

I don't remember applying for the job, but he was very convincing. So here I am, on the threshold of this huge mansion, feeling overwhelmed before I even start.

I've never been in a house this big; I still live with my parents in a three-bedroom bungalow in a safe and quiet part of town. I've got no business being somewhere like this.

I'm about to turn away, get in my car and drive back home, when the door opens.

I expect a butler, but it's Mr. Handsome himself. He's wearing a grey suit that hugs his broad frame, and on one lapel there's a smear of something that looks like it might be banana.

There's a gurgle sound behind him, and he steps aside as his son toddles over on unsteady legs. He scoops him up in an easy motion, and the child squeals with delight.

"He's halfway through his breakfast."

There are no hellos and no niceties. Is this how it's going to be, trading one heartless boss for another? But I need the job, so I plaster on a smile.

"Good morning," I say cheerfully. If he's not going to bring the pleasantries, then I will. "Lovely weather out there."

He frowns at me like I've grown two heads.

"I've got a meeting in five minutes, so if you can get yourself inside, I'll explain Daniel's schedule."

Wow, this guy really has lost the joy of living. I'm tempted to turn on my heel and leave, but this kid reaches out his chubby hand for me and giggles, showing two dimples in his cheeks.

It'd be cruel to leave this happy little boy to the fate of his grumpy father. So I follow him into the house.

The inside is as impressive as the exterior. There's a wide staircase, and I crane my neck trying to see up to the mezzanine. Abstract artwork lines the walls, and a chaise lounge sits in the entry way next to an ornate side table.

I'm pleased to find the kitchen more homely, although still oversized. There's a kitchen island and a solid table with a highchair pulled up next to it. Splashes of food decorate the highchair and the surrounding floor.

"Looks like someone had a good time at breakfast."

He plunks his son down on the floor.

"Lunch is midday and dinner is at 5pm. No cookies, no sweets, nothing to drink but water and milk. He naps straight after lunch. Never let him sleep for more than an hour, or he won't sleep at night. I like him to get fresh air in the morning after breakfast. You can use the garden. There are learning games in the nursery and books. No screens."

I fumble in my bag, looking for a pen to take it down. He produces a piece of paper, neatly typed.

"It's all on here. Any questions?"

Umm, what does he like doing, how do I change a diaper, and does he have a mother somewhere? But he's already turning away, so I keep my mouth shut.

"That all seems straightforward."

"You can go anywhere in the house apart from the top floor. And I have just one rule."

Just the one, I think. Really?

"I like to work in silence. I don't want to hear you or him any more than I have to."

Weird rule for someone who has a toddler in the house, but okay.

"Sure."

He frowns. "Something wrong?"

Yeah, you're behaving like a robot and not a man. "Umm, what if I need you for anything?"

He frowns. "What could you possibly need?"

With that he leaves the kitchen, and I'm left wondering what the hell kind of a man I'm working for now.

3

JAXON

"All the kings' horses and all the kings' men..."

I lean against the doorframe, watching Daniel clap his hands and giggle as Kali sings a nursery rhyme.

Sun comes in the window and falls across her face, making her features glow. She sings with an exaggerated expression that captivates all of Daniel's attention.

Her blonde hair has fallen over her face, and he reaches out a fist to take a chunk of it.

"I don't want my hair pulled today."

She takes his fist gently and plants a kiss on his tubby hand. He giggles at her touch and lunges forward, embracing her in a thick hug.

She lifts him up, laughing, and her eye catches mine. She starts. "I didn't see you there."

It's been a week since I employed the new nanny, and so far she's been satisfactory. My son seems captivated by her, and I want to know what it is he's drawn to.

"We eat lunch together today."

As I head down the hallway, I hear her mutter something under her breath. No doubt a curse at my commanding manner.

It works in my business dealings, but it's hard to turn it off when I leave the virtual boardroom.

Still, she follows me to the kitchen and sets Daniel down in his highchair.

"I'm making garlic honey salmon and Moroccan salad."

"Bit much for a two-year-old."

"Not for Daniel, for us."

She looks startled, and I don't blame her. I've eaten in my office all week, catching up on work from the time I took off.

But I want to get to know my latest employee and find out why she's so goddamn cheerful all the time.

As I make the salad, she feeds Daniel. It's not till she's put him down for his nap and she comes back that I place the food in front of her.

"Would you like wine?"

I choose an Italian Pinot Gris from the wine fridge which perfectly complements the fish. But she shakes her head.

"Probably shouldn't drink on the job. Boss might not like it."

I smile despite myself. She's right. This isn't a date. But I pour myself a generous glass anyway.

"You have a lovely voice."

She looks surprised, and I'm glad I've managed to disarm her. "I heard you singing the nursery rhymes."

"Thank you. I like to sing. I'm in a choir."

She takes a bite of salmon, and her eyes close in pleasure as she chews.

"Mmm, this is good."

Her head tilts up, exposing the soft skin of her throat. I wonder what that skin tastes like, what it would be like to plant soft kisses on her neck...

"I'm surprised you don't have a cook."

Her comment brings me back to reality.

"I like to cook. When I have someone to cook for."

She takes another bite, and we eat in silence for a few moments.

"Do you mind if I ask where Daniel's mother is?"

It's none of her goddamn business, and she must see my wrathful look because she holds her hands up.

"Only because Daniel sometimes calls me momma, and there are no photos of her anywhere, so I'm not sure what I should tell him."

"He's a baby. You don't need to tell him anything."

She chews her salmon quietly, and there's something about her stillness and poise that makes me soften.

"His mother's gone. Left a year ago with a richer man."

Her mouth drops open. "There's a richer man?"

I laugh despite myself. "Yes, that's what you get for marrying a trophy wife; there's always a richer man."

"And she just left her son?"

She sounds incredulous, and I don't blame her. It's against a woman's instincts to leave her own child. But Kali didn't know my heartless ex-wife.

"Unfortunately, yes."

"I'm sorry."

"Don't be. The marriage was a mistake. She was the daughter of a business associate. It was a transaction, not a love match."

It sounds harsh, I know, but that's the truth of it. The biggest mistake of my life, although I got Daniel out of it, so I regret nothing.

I take a large swallow of wine. I don't know why I'm confessing all of this to the nanny. Maybe I'm trying to shock her, but she keeps chewing her lunch, non-judgmental.

"How about you? Tell me about yourself."

She moves her fork around on her plate. "Nothing much to tell. I'm twenty-two years old, and I have no idea what I want to do with my life. My friends have either gone off to college or gotten married, and I'm stuck in Maple Springs doing odd jobs for arrogant bosses. No offense."

"None taken."

She looks contrite, and the way every thought and feeling is plastered across her face is endearing. I'm used to people keeping their thoughts close. It's refreshing to be with someone who's so open.

"Tell me about your family."

She smiles widely and launches into a spiel about her parents. I can tell there's a lot of love there, and I feel a pang of loss for the cold upbringing that I had.

We talk easily for the rest of the lunch. She's guileless and innocent, and she makes me laugh.

It seems like no time at all has passed before Daniel's soft cries come through the baby monitor, and it's time for us both to get back to work.

But as I sit in my office dealing with tough men and hard women, my mind goes back to Kali. Her easy laugh, her quick wit, and the delicate skin of her throat.

4

KALI

I pull the soft blanket up to Daniel's chest and give him a light peck on the cheek. He looks angelic as he sleeps, and my heart fills with love for this little guy.

I didn't know if I could be a nanny, but now I don't know how I couldn't be.

I tiptoe out of Daniel's room, careful not to make a sound, and look around the empty hallway.

For the last two weeks, Mr. Handsome, or Jaxon as he's called, has joined me for lunch most days. He's a surprisingly good cook, and as the days have gone by, he's relaxed slightly and gone from being an uptight, arrogant twat to a semi-normal human being.

I've made it my personal mission to make him laugh, because if anyone needs to lighten up, it's this guy. And I've got to admit, I like the way his eyes crinkle and his face relaxes when he laughs. He goes from being Mr. Handsome to being Mr. Hot Diggity Dog Hot.

Today he's going over some figures for some big business acquisition, so he's taking lunch in his room. After getting Daniel down for his nap, I decide to go and explore.

I've mostly stuck to the lower level of the house apart from the nursery on the second floor. But today it's raining, and I feel restless.

There's a line of doors on either side of the nursery, and the one opposite is open a crack. I push it gently and peer into the room.

It's completely empty. There's a bay window with a window ledge and heavy curtains pulled to the side. I pad into the middle of the room, my feet sinking into the plush carpet.

I stretch my arms out and spin around. There's not a piece of furniture in here and so much free space.

I get a funny feeling in my tummy, wondering what all this space is meant for.

I go to the next room and, feeling bold, push open the door.

It's a mirror of the previous room with a bay window and no furniture.

I try the room across the hall, next to the nursery, and it's the same.

Are these meant to be children's rooms? Left empty, waiting for the sounds of children's laughter and running feet?

I spread my arms out and spin around, imaging the rooms filled with children. For a moment, I imagine they're mine and Mr. Handsome's children. A brood of dark haired, smiling kids running through the corridors, making huts out of the curtains, the walls painted bright and the floor covered with toys.

I close my eyes and a song comes to mind.

My hand runs over the thick curtains as I sing, imagining what it would be like to live forever in this house and make it my own.

5

JAXON

*M*y pen flies across the page as I copy figures from the screen, doing calculations on my notepad. I'm trying to figure out if this proposal will be viable, and my brain hurts from the calculations.

That's when a sound reaches my ears, bringing me out of the complicated math problem I'm trying to figure out. It's the sweet sound of singing, and it breaks my concentration. I try to get back to the figures, but the song fills my head and I've lost the numbers.

"Damn." I throw my pen down in frustration, and it skitters across the desk and onto the floor. The nub breaks, and ink spills onto the cream carpet.

"Damn that girl."

I'm seething as I head downstairs and to the next level. The singing's coming from one of the spare rooms and I push the door open, ready to give her a piece of my mind.

I stop in my tracks.

Kali is standing with her arms outstretched facing the window. Her face is tilted up to the sun which glints off her blonde hair, giving her a glow like an angel.

She's singing a sweet, slow song that makes the hairs on my arms stand up.

I freeze, unable to move as I watch and listen to her.

After a few moments she must sense my presence, because she stops abruptly and turns around.

I came here to tell her off, and as I close the distance between us, I do just that.

"I told you to be silent while I'm working."

Her mouth drops open and there's an apology on her lips, but I don't give her time to speak. My arm slides around her waist and she tilts her head up to me, her eyes wide in surprise.

"You've broken my concentration and ruined my carpet."

Her face is inches from mine and she looks startled, but she doesn't pull away.

"Sorry," she whispers.

I press my lips against hers, and they're soft and fresh and I can still taste the song on them. It's a slow kiss, and when I break away she's breathing hard.

"Do that again," she says, and I oblige.

This time the kiss is intense, insistent. I run my hands over her back, her ass, pulling her against me.

My dick thickens, and I know that I want her. I want her innocence, her joy for life. I want to tie myself to that.

Her chest heaves up and down, and I flick my eyes to her breasts and the delicate skin of her throat.

My mouth closes over her throat and she gasps, a sound that is magnified in this empty room.

"Shhh." I place a hand over her mouth. "Don't make another sound."

Sweet Jesus, he's kissing me and it feels freakin' fantastic.

"Don't make another sound."

His hand closes over my mouth, and it's terrifying and the biggest turn-on of my life. My panties dampen, and my breathing gets shallow.

He shuffles me backwards and pushes me against the wall, his body pressing against mine. His hard cock rubs against me, and there's no hiding his intentions.

My eyes must go wide, because a look of concern slices across his face.

"Tell me if you don't want this?"

I give him a look, because his hands over my mouth and I can't tell him anything. Instead I press myself against him, rubbing my pelvis into his hips.

His eyes roll backward for a moment before they find mine again.

"I'm going to fuck you, Kali."

Oh sweet Jesus, my panties have melted.

"If you want me to, nod your head."

I just about strain my neck I'm nodding so vigorously.

"Good. But my son is asleep on the other side of this wall, so I can't have you make a sound."

I nod again, and he releases his hand. It immediately slides south and hikes up my skirt.

He runs a hand over my damp panties, and my pussy throbs under his touch. He pulls at the fabric, ripping my panties in his haste. His fingers run over my pussy lips, and I let out a moan.

His hand immediately covers my mouth again.

"I said to be quiet."

It should be annoying, being told off like a child, but his gruff voice and commanding manner make my want him even more.

This time he keeps his hand over my mouth as he pulls at his pants with his other hand. His dick pops out, and it's thick and long and I stifle a gasp at the sight of it.

He kisses my throat as he pulls at my skirt, causing a delicious sensation to course through my body. I feel the tip of his dick graze my opening, and I breath heavily under his hand.

"Not a sound," he whispers as he puts the tip of his cock inside me. I suppress a moan, and his eyes meet mine.

"Good girl."

Holy shit, this is exquisite torture. Not being able to make a noise intensifies my other senses and makes me squirm in a good way.

He eases in another inch, and I let out a moan into his palm.

He freezes and I whimper, wanting him to keep going.

"You make a noise and this stops." He slides his dick almost fully out of me, and I almost beg for him to put it back in. But I've learned my lesson and keep quiet.

He must see the pleading look in my eyes, because he smiles.

"You're getting the idea."

I don't question why he's allowed to whisper and I'm not even allowed a moan. Right now, all I can think about is getting his girth inside my eager pussy.

Slowly, so slowly, he slides himself into me. My head tilts back against the wall, and I fight the urge to cry out.

His free hand grabs my ass and he lifts me up from the wall, angling my hips as he thrusts all the way inside me.

My mouth opens in a silent cry as he fills me up. It feels so good that I want to cry out, but his hand is over my mouth, and repressing the noise makes the feeling more intense.

He keeps his eyes on mine and his hand firmly over my mouth as he thrusts into me, short sharp movements that push me against the wall with every thrust.

His face is determined, and his gaze never leaves mine.

"Not," he thrusts, "a" another thrust, "sound."

Fuuccck! I want to cry out. I want to sing his name from the rafters. It's so intense.

I press my mouth again his palm, my cries stifled by his rough hand. My hips buck with him as he slams into me.

Then I'm climaxing, I bite down on his palm and he jerks into me, his body rigid as he comes.

It's only after I stop trembling that I let out a whimper. He lowers his hand and brushes my lips with his.

"Good girl."

He kisses me tenderly.

I'm in a daze. What the hell just happened? I just had weird silent sex with my boss. Surely that's a bad move. But I feel freakin' fantastic. I feel a connection with him. It's been building all week, and this feels like it was inevitable.

I'm straightening my skirt up when he tilts my head up. His eyes find mine.

"Kali…" At that moment, there's a cry from down the hall.

He goes still as we listen to Daniel waking up. I wait for Jaxon to say whatever he was going to say, but he doesn't.

"Daniel's awake." I state the obvious. We stare at

each other for a moment before I realize he's not going to say anything.

I smooth my hair down, and as I turn to leave he catches my arm.

I turn expectantly, waiting for him to say something, to tell me he feels this connection too, that I haven't just given myself up for a quickie with the boss, but he just squeezes my hand.

"You'd better go get the baby."

I stumble to the door on legs that are still wobbly. What the hell have I just done?

Daniel's whimpers propel me down the hall, but I make a quick stop in the bathroom to wash my hands.

As I look at myself in the mirror, pink, rosy cheeks and hair messed up, I can't help the grin that spreads across my face.

That was the most delectable sex I've ever had. But it's not just that. I feel something for this man. Something that's stirred in me over the last few weeks, as I've watched how tender he is with his son, as we've chatted over lunch, as I've made him laugh, cracking through his tough exterior.

"It was just sex," I tell my refection. "Don't get too excited."

But my heart knows it wasn't just sex. I know it was more than that.

7

JAXON

*K*ali comes into the kitchen with Daniel and I step quickly past them and out the door, swiping my plate of food on the way out.

"Just a sandwich today, is it?"

She says it casually, but I hear the sharp edge to her voice. It's been a week since our encounter, and I've been avoiding her since.

I'm not proud of myself. And I know I'm behaving like an asshole. But she's stirred up feelings in me that have no place in my heart.

I stop by the door and watch her put Daniel in his highchair. Her damned hair falls in golden waves down her back, and I long to run my hands through it.

"I've got an important meeting at two, so make sure you get him up early and both keep quiet."

She straightens up and looks me dead in the eye. "I'm good at not making a sound."

She says it softly and I'm instantly transported back to being inside her, her hot pussy around my cock and her soft body in my arms.

My dick rises to attention, and I turn away before she can see the effect she has on me.

I hear her sigh as I walk down the hall.

It would be so easy to take her in my arms again and fuck her senseless. But there's a warning pang in my heart. It's not just sex with Kali. It's something more. And I'm not ready for that ever again.

It's later that evening, and I come downstairs to relieve Kali of her shift. Daniel's already in bed, and she's waiting in the living room reading a magazine.

She stands up when I enter the room, and there's something in her demeanor that sets alarm bells ringing.

"Report."

She tells me the details of Daniel's day like she does at the end of every shift. I nod, but I'm only half listening.

I go to the cabinet and pour myself a glass of bourbon.

"Drink?"

She shakes her head. There's no joke this time, and I feel a pang of regret. I miss her quick wit.

I sip my drink, but I'm watching her like a hawk as she gives me her report. Her hair is tied up in a messy bun that's slipped sideways throughout the day, no doubt from my son pulling on it. There's a food stain on her t-shirt right over the left breast.

I'd like to rip that t-shirt off and explore her body properly.

She stops talking but she's fidgeting with her hands and I get the feeling there's something else she wants to say.

I put my glass down. "What is it?"

She clears her throat. "I can't work here anymore. I resign."

It's like a blow to the stomach. I've gotten used to her in my house, the soft notes of her singing, the scent of her body wash that lingers in the rooms long after she's gone, the giggles from my son when he's with her.

"You can't resign. Daniel has gotten used to you."

She gives me an indignant look and her hands go to her hips.

"Don't try to use Daniel to make me stay. We both know why I have to leave."

"You're the best nanny my son has ever had."

"You should have thought of that before you mauled me last week."

I stand up and close the distance between us. "Is that what it felt like? A mauling?"

She swallows hard, and my eyes flick to her throat. I feel my pulse race, and I want to kiss her so bad.

"No," she whispers.

"Because I recall you liked it."

She's breathing hard, and I'm about to kiss her when she steps back, her hand coming up in front of her.

"I'm not something you can just take when you want, Jaxon, just because you're rich."

The words are like a punch to the guts. Is this really what she thinks of me?

"It's not like that, Kali."

"Yeah? Then why haven't you spoken to me all week?"

"I have."

She shakes her head, exasperated. "You've asked for my reports on your son, and that's about it."

"I know I've behaved badly, but come here and let me make it up to you."

I take a step toward her, and she takes another step back.

"And then what? I become your nanny and fuck buddy? I deserve more than that."

She's right. She deserves love and happiness and a man who will love her with a whole heart, not a cold man like me.

"I thought there was something between us. I was wrong."

She's breathing heavily and looking at me expectantly, waiting for me to contradict her. But I can't. I won't be taken in by another woman, and I won't open my heart again.

After a few moments, her look turns to sad resignation and it almost breaks my heart. I want to kiss her, make her happy again, but I stand stricken dumb as she picks up her bag.

"Goodbye, Mr. Handsome."

I don't say anything as she leaves, and a few moments later I hear the front door open and close. I sink onto the couch as I hear her engine start and she drives away.

I should feel relief that my heart dodged a heartbreak. But all I feel is empty.

8

KALI

I run my cloth over the counter and try not to cringe as Steve leans on the bar next to me. His eyes slide down to my chest, and he doesn't even bother trying to lift them back to my face.

"After you've done a round of the tables, the trash needs taking out."

"Sure."

He finally glances up at my face, and his eyes narrow. "And put a smile on, will ya? The customers like to see a pretty girl smile."

It hurt my pride to come back to Steve and beg for a job, but there wasn't anything else around, and better the devil you know, right? At least Steve never tried to use his position to have sex with me.

My mind flashes back to being pressed against the wall, Jaxon's hand covering my mouth. I sigh at the memory. Whether he abused his position or not, I'll never regret that quickie against the wall.

I was sure there was something more to it. I'm still not sure how I got it so wrong, thinking there was a real connection when it was just sex he was after. I was sure he was into me.

But what do I know of the whims of the rich? I guess it was all a ruse to get in my pants.

The single dad support group is in tonight, with Jaxon noticeably absent. I give them a wide berth. The last thing I need is to attract the attention of another single dad looking to get laid.

I head to the opposite side of the room to wipe down the booths. I'm clearing a table when I hear footsteps behind me.

When I turn around, Jaxon is standing watching me. His hair is mused up and there's stubble on his chin, which is rough for him. He's usually clean shaven and well put together, but damn it, it makes him look even hotter. My heart soars despite myself, and there's a hopeful fluttering in my chest.

"Daniel misses you."

Trust Jaxon to get straight to the point. He's come here for his son, not to tell me I was wrong. I turn away to hide my disappointment and get busy wiping down the booth.

"I'm not coming back to nanny for you."

"I don't want you to."

Wow, talk about harsh. "Good. That's settled."

He reaches out a hand and stops my wrist. His touch is electric, and I suppress a gasp. I don't want him to see what effect he has on me.

"I didn't speak to you after we made love because I was afraid."

"Afraid I'd sue you for gross misconduct."

"No. I was afraid of what I was feeling."

Now I'm listening.

"When my wife left me, I swore I'd never marry again."

"Whoa, I wasn't asking for marriage. Just a little bit of common curtesy."

He lets go of my wrist and runs his fingers through his hair. I get back to wiping the table.

"I'm sorry I behaved badly."

I turn to face him and take a really good look at him. For once there's no hardness to his expression; his eyes are soft and open and vulnerable. And he looks rough. There are bags under his eyes, and his complexion is sallow.

I want to be cross with him, but I find I no longer have it in me.

"Apology accepted. Can I get back to my job now?"

He's looking at me intensely. "But I feel things for you, Kali. I thought I could let you go and protect my heart, but the truth is I'm miserable without you. I want you, Kali, not just your body. I want you in my life. Permanently."

I can't breathe. Everything he's saying proves that my instincts weren't wrong.

"I swore I'd never marry again, but what I should have sworn is that I'd never marry without love. And I love you, Kali."

My heart stops in my chest. Mr. Handsome just confessed his love for me.

"Are you serious?"

He takes a step closer, and this time I don't back away.

"I'm always serious."

His lips curl up at the sides, and I realize that's his attempt at a joke. Because yeah, he is always serious.

"Come back to the house. Not as my nanny, but as my woman."

Oh my, who can resist a line like that? My knees go wobbly, and I drop my cleaning cloth.

"Okay." It comes out as a squeak, but it's enough to make his face light up.

His arm slides around my waist, and he pulls me toward him. I tilt my head back, and he kisses me long and hard.

A cheer erupts from the other side of the bar, and we break away as the single dad support group cheers and claps.

They raise their drinks to us as Jaxon pulls me close. He's got a smile on his face, and I feel warm inside knowing that I put it there.

Suddenly my purpose in life becomes clear. It's not

working in dead end jobs. My purpose is being right here with him. Bringing joy and laughter and song into his serious world.

"Let's get out of here."

I pull off my apron and throw it down on the table.

"This time I won't be back."

EPILOGUE

KALI

Six years later…

"Here you go, sweetie. Mommy will be back in a few hours."

I hand the baby over to the nanny and make my exit out of the nursery.

My three-year-old toddles after me, and I give her a hug before directing her back into the playroom.

The nanny distracts her, and I make my escape up the stairs.

My kids are my world, and I know it's a luxury, but having a nanny three days a week lets me get some time to myself so I can go to choir practice, and some time with my husband.

I push the door to his office open quietly and poke my head around the door.

He looks up with a frown, and his expression immediately softens when he sees me.

"You're not in a meeting?"

He pushes his chair away from the desk.

"Nope."

"The kids are with the nanny. Did you want to have lunch together today?"

His gaze runs lazily over my chest, and I feel my body awaken at his look.

"I'm feeling hungry for something."

My heart rate quickens as he moves toward me. His smooth skin grazes mine as he captures my lips in a passionate kiss.

"I've got five minutes before my next meeting."

Already his fingers are in my panties, running over the damp fabric and causing a ripple of desire through my body.

"We'd better be quick then."

He grunts as I pull at his belt buckle, sliding his cock out of his pants and into my hands.

"Shhh," I warn him. "Don't make a sound."

He smiles at the memory of our first time.

"I won't if you won't."

He pushes me against the wall and lifts my skirt around my hips. His hand goes over my mouth, and I stifle a gasp. His dick probes my opening, and I guide him in with my hands.

As he sinks into me I long to cry out, but I keep my mouth shut, enjoying the exquisite torture.

I lift my leg and he grabs my thigh, holding it up so he can sink deep into me.

It doesn't take long before we're both climaxing, gripping each other in our silent pleasure.

Afterward I fix my skirts, and then give him a kiss and leave him to his meeting.

I know he'll finish early today, and we'll go pick Daniel up from school together. I'll help Daniel with his homework while Jaxon fixes dinner.

There'll be chaos while we get the little ones to bed, and then we'll have quiet time together. We might make love again, this time slowly while our babies sleep soundly.

I have a purpose in life now, and it's my family.

WILD HEART MOUNTAIN: MILITARY HEROES

He's a scarred military hero. She's the young, innocent woman forced to spend a night in his cabin...

My unit came back to Wild Heart Mountain to heal and to hide. I've been doing a lot of hiding until I meet Hailey.

I'm scarred, I'm damaged, and I'm way too old for her. But the curvy and quirky Hailey makes me feel alive. She brings hope and joy back to my life.

I faced the enemy in Iraq, but it's nothing compared to the vulnerability I feel when Hailey holds my heart in her hands. Can she see past the scars, the limp, and the age gap, or was it pity that brought her to my bed?

Loved by the Mountain Man is a forced proximity, ex-military, age gap, instalove romance featuring a scarred military mountain man and the curvy, innocent heroine who may be the healing balm that this damaged hero needs.

Keep reading for an excerpt.

LOVED BY THE MOUNTAIN MAN

CHAPTER ONE

Kobe

Dark clouds envelop the mountain as I pull into the parking lot of Angie's Bar. My knee twinges as I climb out of my pickup and I rub it absently, trying to get blood into the damaged tissue. If I didn't already know by the clouds, my bad leg is a pretty good barometer of when it's going to snow.

It's not a good night to be out, but I never miss a vets night with the former Marines from my old unit.

If I didn't organize these monthly meet ups, I doubt some of them would come down the mountain at all. The mountains are a good place for hiding and healing, which is why so many of us ended up back here on Wild Heart Mountain.

Some days I'm not sure which one I'm doing.

A blast of warm air greets me as I cross the

threshold of Angie's Bar. She's got the fire blasting even though the place is almost empty. I make a mental note to bring more firewood next time I'm in town. She'll need it if she has the fire going every night.

A couple of the guys are ready at a table near the dartboard. I give them a nod before heading to the bar.

Angie gives me a tired smile. "Looks like snow tonight."

I give her a quick peck on the cheek, and when I look up, Corbin's eyeing me with his brows furrowed.

I tilt my hand to my mouth, silently asking if he needs another drink.

He gives me a nod and keeps his eyes on us.

If I didn't know Corbin better, I'd probably be terrified of his intense looks. But quiet and brooding is just his way.

Angie's kids are at a booth in the restaurant area with homework spread out on the table. And aside from our group, there's only one other table of diners.

It's worrying how empty the place is. I grew up with Angie and her husband. He was the only one in our unit who didn't come home.

She struggles with this place, not that she'd ever admit it. Her family opened the bar back in the nineties and named it after her. When we were kids, this was the only bar in town and the center of the community. It got run down over the years, and Angie and Paul were going to bring it back to life.

They did some renovations every time he was back

on leave, and his plan was to retire from the military and help her run the place.

Now she's stuck with a half renovated bar and two kids to raise on her own.

Any of us would step up to help out Paul's widow, but she won't accept money from us. So we find other ways to help.

Which is why I brought my tool kit in with me.

"Where's the door that needs fixing?" I ask.

"Upstairs. Damn lock's broken, and I've got a tenant."

My eyebrows raise in surprise. Angie's got a spare room above the bar that she rents out on short lease. It's easy to find tenants during the tourist season, but with winter coming there aren't many travelers to the mountain.

"She's a young girl who's helping me out at the bar for a few weeks. She's not in town for much longer, but I can't have her staying with a door that doesn't lock."

I wonder what kind of crazy kid comes to the mountain in winter. But it's extra income for Angie, so thank God for the crazies.

"I'll say hello to the boys, then I'll head up."

At that moment, one of her kids comes running over. Her hair is wild, there's a hole in her woolen sweater, and her shoes look almost worn. It breaks my heart to see Paul's kids like this. But Angie's too proud to take cash.

"Hey, sweetheart." I bend down so I'm level with the

little girl. Fran is five years old and doesn't remember her Daddy. I slide a twenty-dollar bill into her hand.

"Go share this with your brother."

The little girl's face lights up.

"Can I spend it on candy?" She looks up at her mom with hope in her dark eyes.

Angie gives me a grateful look. "Of course you can, sweetheart."

The little girl throws her arms around my neck. "Thank you, Uncle Kobe."

Then she skips off, waving the bill excitedly to show her brother.

I pull myself up, ignoring the protest from my leg.

"You shouldn't have." But Angie's giving me a thankful look.

"You know, I'll be more than happy to help. If you need money for winter clothes or anything…"

It's useless trying to finish. Angie's already shaking her head. Her damn mountain pride won't let her take a handout.

"Thanks, Kobe. You do enough already. You guys all do. I've had Corbin in all week cutting firewood for me. And he fixed my car, which saves me a trip to the mechanic. I appreciate all that you guys do, really."

It's been over four years since she lost her husband, and I know how hard that was on her, but I never see Angie complain. At least she's got the bar to keep her busy, and the kids are a comfort. Paul was loved by everybody here. No one's gonna let his widow and kids go without.

"Wrap up warm tonight. That snow's gonna get bad."

"I will."

The guys have chosen a table in the darkest corner of the bar, which is no surprise. My former Marine buddies gravitate to the shadows. Even if the dartboard wasn't over here, they'd still find the darkest corner to sit in.

Rhys was the one that got us all into darts while we were on tour. He got a board from somewhere, and we set it up in the mess. Then he'd thrash us night after night, hitting straight bullseyes.

He was good, could have gone professional if he'd wanted to. He tells us it was from a misspent youth.

Rhys is focused on the dartboard. His hands are trembling, but we all ignore it, since that's what he's doing.

That's what life is when you return from war. You have to learn to live with the things you brought back with you. Reframe your life to incorporate the damages.

To reiterate my thoughts, my leg gives a twinge, and I grit my teeth. I've gotten used to walking with a limp, but I don't like anyone seeing how much it pains me.

Rhys takes the shot and it hits just off the bullseye.

"Nice shot, man," Corbin says.

Rhys just grunts and grabs one of the beers I've set on the table.

Sometimes when we were on tour, we'd put bets on how many bullseyes he'd get in a night. I haven't seen him get one since we've been back.

The fact that he's still playing is a testament to the man's tenacity. A lesser man might have given up, but not Rhys. When there's something he wants, he won't stop till he gets it.

Rhys is intense and brooding, just like Corbin. He was the deadliest sniper in our platoon. He could creep up on anyone. The man still scares the bejesus out of me.

He guzzles his beer, and I'm wondering if he's trying to see if alcohol can stop the tremors.

My phone buzzes in my pocket, and it's a message from Dylan, telling me he's not going to make it because his babysitter fell through.

Dylan must have been through every willing babysitter on the mountain. But he's a grumpy son of a bitch, and there aren't many babysitters willing to trek that far into the mountain to his remote cabin.

Dylan left the military when his wife passed, and he's never forgiven himself for not being there for her. I was hoping he would be here tonight. Social contact is good for these guys, but I have to practically pull them out of their cabins sometimes. Like I said, it's a great place to heal, and a great place to hide.

The door busts open and Symon strides through,

stomping his boots on the mat and clapping his hands together.

"Snow's started."

His voice booms across the room, causing the table of diners to pause in their meals and look up. Symon gives them a friendly nod and a wave.

As a volunteer Ranger, he's gotten to know quite a few people around the town and is the only one of us that doesn't seem to mind human interaction.

"Sorry I'm late, guys." He slides into a chair next to me, and I hand him a beer.

"A couple of tourists got lost," Symon continues. "With the snowstorm coming it was all hands on deck to find them." Symon shakes his head in mock disgust. "Damn tourists. Who goes hiking when there's a storm coming?"

"Who comes out to a bar when there's a storm coming?" quips Corbin.

"Touché." Symon holds his beer up, and we all knock bottles. "I didn't want to miss your ugly mugs."

Symon's the joker of the group, and lord knows we all need that.

He launches into an account of his afternoon tracking down tourists, gesticulating wildly and making even Corbin crack a smile, almost.

The windowpane rattles, drawing my attention to how the wind's picked up.

"Hate to say it fellas, but we should probably eat and go."

Corbin pushes his chair away and stands up. "I'll ask Angie to get the pizzas on."

We always come to Angie's, and we always order more food than we need and take the leftovers home in doggie bags. It's another little way we can help support her.

While we're waiting for the food, I head upstairs to fix the door. With the storm coming in, I'll want to get away as soon as we've eaten. Not ideal, but when you live on a mountain you learn to respect the weather.

There's no hiding the pain in my leg as I drag it up the metal stairs outside that are already covered in a thin layer of snow. It's slow going with my toolbox in one hand, and I'm glad none of the guys can see how slow I've become. How much less of a man I am than the one that lead our unit in Iraq.

As I make my way up the steps, I realize I never asked the name of Angie's tenant.

LOVED BY THE MOUNTAIN MAN

CHAPTER TWO

Hailey

Hot water gushes over me as I rinse the conditioner out of my hair. I give my hips a little shake as I belt out the chorus to Sweet Home Alabama. There's something about being on the road that's got me singing all the big American hits.

I haven't even been to Alabama. Yet. It's on my hit list.

It's been two months since I left Sanborne, my small hometown in rural Virginia. I'm working my way down the east coast states and around the bottom of the Appalachian Mountains to see what's on the other side. Coming from Virginia, I've spent some time in the mountains before. But my travels of the last few months have really opened me up to their beauty. I can see why people come to the mountains of North Carolina, especially Wild Heart Mountain. It's absolutely breathtaking.

I quickly rinse the last of the conditioner out of my hair and turn the shower off. Angie has been a great landlord for these last two weeks, and I don't want to use more hot water than necessary. Any single mom running a business and raising two kids on their own needs all the help they can get. I've been working the bar for her and helping out with odd jobs, but she's given me tonight off and I don't intend to waste it.

I'm washing my hair, I'm going to put on a face mask, make myself cheesy pasta, and veg out in front of the TV. It's a small box TV and there's no cable, but I found a channel that's playing The Bachelor at 9 o'clock. I've got a date. Me, the TV, and cheesy pasta.

I feel a pang of sadness that Trish isn't here to watch it with me. I always watch The Batchelor with my sister, but other than that, it's a pretty perfect night.

I read somewhere that two weeks is the optimal time to stay in a transitory job, so that's how long I told Angie I was staying for. She was grateful for the help, and I accepted minimum wage because I could see she couldn't afford much else.

I get the room for free and a hot meal every day. It's not much, but it's enough for the bus fare to the next town and a few nights' accommodation if I don't find work immediately. Luckily the entertainment is free around here. On my days off, I've been wandering the trails in the mountains taking in the wildlife and the beauty.

It's low tourist season, but plenty of places need help redecorating or deep cleaning in the off season.

I'm happy to turn my hand to anything. On the road I've tried cleaning, painting, nannying, bar work, mending fences, turning soil, and looking after pigs. The smell got to me on that last one.

But I still haven't found my purpose in life, which is what this whole trip is about.

My sister Trish and all my friends were happy to stay in Sanborne and have babies, but I'm sure there's more to life than that. I just don't know what yet.

Mom never exactly talked to us about a career, and going to college wasn't something anyone in our family does. I'm not sure I want to go and study for years anyway, even if I knew what I wanted to do. I'm hoping by travelling around I'll find my calling, my purpose in life. And it definitely won't be having babies and hooking up with a small-town man who expects me to cook and clean for him for the rest of his life.

No way. I want more out of life than that.

I'm singing at the top of my lungs as my towel shimmies over my wide ass when I hear a noise in the apartment. It might be Angie bringing up a pizza for dinner. She's good like that. I don't know if it's because she feels like she has to mother me, but I am definitely leaning into that.

I wrap the towel around me and pull open the bathroom door just as there's a loud crash.

My apartment door is wide open, and there's a man standing there. He's silhouetted against the single streetlight from the parking lot below. He looks as big as the mountain, and he's carrying an axe.

I scream.

This is what my sister warned me about when I told her I was going travelling. She warned me I'd get murdered in some small town.

The man is so big he takes up the whole door frame, his broad shoulders barely fitting in the doorway. His coat hangs open, giving me a peek of a tight T-shirt and a hint of muscles, which is weird. I didn't expect an axe murderer to be wielding such defined pecs. You never see that in the horror movies.

The man takes a step towards me, and I scream again. There's a snow globe of the mountain sitting on the dresser, and I pick it up and launch it at him.

Unfortunately, sport has never been my strong suit.

The snow globe goes so wide he doesn't even duck. It misses the man completely and smashes through the window beside the door. The tinkling sound of breaking glass fills the silence.

"I suppose I'm gonna have to fix that window too."

His voice is as low and rumbly as the dark clouds rolling in off the mountain and sends my nipples into hard peaks.

Axe murderers are never this sexy in the films.

But instead of moving toward me, the man-mountain slowly drops the axe. Now that I look at it properly, it's not an axe. It's a bright yellow toolbox.

He raises his hands in a placating gesture. Big hands. Rough hands. Working man's hands with calluses. The thought of those rough hands running over my skin and snagging on my nipples fills my brain so utterly that for a moment I can only gape at them.

"You're Angie's tenant, right?"

There's that voice again, low and rumbling, sending tremors through my body and causing my own personal earthquake.

He knows Angie, and I'm beginning to think he's not here to murder me.

His eyes flick down my body. My body that's only covered in a towel.

It's a big body. I'm not complaining, but the towels here are threadbare and barely bigger than a dishcloth.

I pull the towel tighter around me, unsuccessfully attempting to cover all of my curves.

Yes," I squeak.

"I'm Kobe," the mountain man says. "Angie sent me to fix your door. And I guess you want that window fixed too?"

My racing heart starts to calm. He's not here to ravish me and murder me. A little part of me feels disappointed. Not at the murdering part, but a ravishing by this man? That's something I could get behind, or under as the case may be.

As realization sets in that I've just thrown a snow globe at a very sexy man who's come to do some building maintenance, my cheeks flush.

"Umm. Yeah. The lock's broken," I say with as much dignity as a large girl in a towel the size of a postage stamp can muster. His eyes travel down my body, and I flush under his gaze.

I'm a curvy girl and I love my body, but I can't help wondering what this man thinks of me. By the time he's taking to look me over, I have a suspicion he's quite partial to curvy girls. Or maybe there aren't many women on the mountain, and he is still thinking of ravishing me. My nipples perk up hopefully at the thought.

"Mind if I get to work?"

I realize I'm still staring at him, and heat rises to my cheeks.

"Sure," I squeak. "I'm just gonna get changed."

It's a studio apartment, and the bed takes up one wall. My open bag lies on the floor between the bed and the door, right next to Kobe.

His gaze follows mine, and the heat intensifies in my cheeks. My underwear is strewn on top of my open bag. White cotton panties with a lace trim. I snatch up the panties and quickly grab some other clothes and scurry back into the bathroom, shutting the door firmly behind me. I lean on the back of the door, needing to breathe.

I don't know if it's the heating on full bore or the sexy definitely-not-an-axe-murderer man out there, but it's suddenly burning hot in this place.

To keep reading visit:
mybook.to/LovedbytheMountainMan

GET YOUR FREE BOOK

Sign up to the Sadie King mailing list for a FREE book!

You'll be the first to hear about exclusive offers, bonus content and all the news from Sadie King.

To claim your free book visit:
www.authorsadieking.com/free

BOOKS BY SADIE KING

Wild Heart Mountain

Wild Heart Mountain: Military Heroes

Wild Heart Mountain: Wild Riders MC

Sunset Coast

Underground Crows MC

Sunset Security

Men of the Sea

The Thief's Lover

The Henchman's Obsession

The Hitman's Redemption

Maple Springs

Men of Maple Mountain

All the Single Dads

Candy's Café

Small Town Sisters

For a full list of titles check out the Sadie King website

www.authorsadieking.com

Sadie King is a USA Today Best Selling Author of short instalove romance.

She lives in New Zealand with her ex-military husband and raucous young son.

When she's not writing she loves catching waves with her son, running along the beach, and good wine, preferably drunk with a book in hand.

Keep in touch when you sign up for her newsletter. You'll even snag yourself a free short romance!

www.authorsadieking.com/free

www.ingramcontent.com/pod-product-compliance
Lightning Source LLC
Chambersburg PA
CBHW051303160726
47994CB00003B/1299